中国古诗欣赏（中级篇）
Appreciation of Chinese Ancient Poems (Intermediate)

主　编　丁　丽　范志坚
副主编　王树娟　李庆建　何　玉
　　　　杨　帆　陈莹莹　阎文欣
　　　　马英骁　司徒一焯　张秀花
英文翻译　仇全菊
插图绘制　王宗香

中国海洋大学出版社
·青岛·

图书在版编目（CIP）数据

中国古诗欣赏：中级篇 / 丁丽，范志坚主编．－－
青岛：中国海洋大学出版社，2021.11
　　ISBN 978-7-5670-2952-1

Ⅰ.①中… Ⅱ.①丁…②范… Ⅲ.①古典诗歌－诗集－中国 Ⅳ.①I222.72

中国版本图书馆 CIP 数据核字（2021）第 205832 号

出版发行	中国海洋大学出版社			
社　　址	青岛市香港东路 23 号	邮政编码	266071	
出 版 人	杨立敏			
网　　址	http://pub.ouc.edu.cn			
电子信箱	184385208@qq.com			
订购电话	0532-82032573（传真）			
责任编辑	付绍瑜	电　　话	0532-85902533	
印　　制	青岛中苑金融安全印刷有限公司			
版　　次	2021 年 11 月第 1 版			
印　　次	2021 年 11 月第 1 次印刷			
成品尺寸	170 mm×230 mm			
印　　张	8.25			
字　　数	70 千			
印　　数	1～1 000			
定　　价	40.00 元			

发现印装质量问题，请致电 0532-85662115，由印刷厂负责调换。

第一课 梅

第二课 春

第三课 江

第四课　鸟

苍苍竹林寺

杳杳钟声晚

荷笠带斜阳

青山独归远

刘长卿

第五课　送

第六课 剑

君自故鄉來
應知故鄉事
來日綺窗前
寒梅著花未

王維

第七课 乡

第八课　愁

第九课 客

第十课　母

第十一课 望

第十二课　雨

第十三课　山

第十四课　题

第十五课　别

  本教材为中文非母语的学习者编写,主要面向来华学习的国际学生,适用于其中文、中国古诗欣赏、中华文化和中国概况等课程。本教材收录了15首五言古诗,每首诗配有辅助学习者理解的水墨画、古诗知识和许渊冲先生的英文翻译;按绝句到律诗的顺序由浅入深;选取的古诗篇幅短小,韵律感强,以写景和写人为主,抒情为辅;教材的练习环节强调趣味性、任务性和活动化。本册教材难度大致对应《国际中文教育中文水平等级标准》的中等等级。教材初稿完成后,已在山东科技大学学历生和非学历生中进行了多次教学实验,并结合教学效果和使用反馈进行了修改。

  衷心感谢美国佛蒙特大学亚洲语言文学系主任印京华教授、山东科技大学外国语学院姜泗平教授。两位教授提出的具体建议和意见使本教材得以不断完善。

  感谢教材初稿试用期间山东科技大学国际学生积极反馈使用感受和提供建议。也敬请读者朋友提出宝贵意见,在此一并致谢!

序言

  诗是一种具有节奏和韵律的语言艺术,用以表达情感,阐述心灵,反映生活,引发共鸣。中国由于汉语语言本身独有的特点以及延绵不断的悠久文化历史而成为诗的国度。

  汉语语言本身有什么特点使中国成为诗的国度呢?从汉语发音来看,有三个主要特点:(1)一个汉字一个音节;(2)每个音节都以元音或元音加鼻辅音来结尾,没有以除鼻辅音以外的辅音来结尾的音节;(3)每个音节都带有声调。一字一音使汉语易于富有节奏;音节结尾都是元音或元音加鼻辅音,使汉语不仅发音比较响亮,而且更易于押韵;每个音节都带有声调,使汉语更富有音乐性。汉语这些得天独厚的特点成为中国诗人得心应手的工具。

  中国是诗的国度与其延绵不断的悠久文化历史有什么关系呢?早在2 500年前,中国最早深受敬重的教育家孔子(公元前551—前479年)就用选自其前500年间由王公贵族、文人雅士、平民百姓创作的诗歌编纂而成的《诗经》作为教材教化学生。中国的诗自此随着中国历史的进程持续发展起来。楚辞、汉赋、汉乐府、唐诗、宋词、元曲,等等,成为各个重要历史时期中国古诗发展的标志性体裁并流传至今。其中尤以唐诗最为典型。中国唐代(公元618—907年)延续了选拔辅佐朝政人才的科举考试。写诗的能力成为科举考试中的重要考核项目。除了业已存在的古体诗,当时又产生了像绝句和律诗这样对格律和韵律有严格要求的近体诗。大约800年之后,于公元1705年成书的《全唐诗》收录了2 300多名唐代诗人所写的48 900多首诗,内容涵盖了人们生活中的方方面面。

人类历史上还没有哪个国家、哪个历史时代能产生这么多的诗人并写出这么多的诗吧。无论古体诗还是近体诗,都因创作时间的久远,可统称为古诗。由于古诗朗朗上口、富有美感、不乏智慧、情趣盎然,在当代中国,无论男女老幼,大都能脱口而出,吟诵几句。诗已深深融入中国人精神文化生活中。

  对来自其他国家和文化的学生来说,要体验中国文化,要了解中国人的情趣,学习、理解、诵读、欣赏中国古诗不失为一个有趣、有益又给力的方式。丁丽老师以她在中国诗词歌赋方面的学识修养和国际中文教学方面的实践经验精心编写了这本《中国古诗欣赏(中级篇)》,内容丰富,编排有序。书中一共有15课,每课用一个字作为题目,简洁地标示出该课的主题。每课根据主题,配有精选出的一首五言古诗,并附有诗人创作该诗的背景简况。为方便学生朗诵,每首五言诗都有汉语拼音的标注。为帮助学生感受和欣赏诗意,每首五言诗都提供了许渊冲先生的英语翻译,还配有一幅有王宗香老师绘制的插画。为确保学生理解诗意,每课都对五言诗的诗句逐行用现代汉语和英语进行了双语复述,并根据诗中出现的新字词提供了生词表。有关古诗的常识,每课有重点地介绍一个。书中每一课既有对古诗诗意的讲解,也有针对诗格式的简单练习,以及与诗中内容相关话题的开展讨论的问题。每课的最后,作为阅读的扩展,还精选了三首与这一课主题相关的古诗,供学生欣赏。

  《中国古诗欣赏(中级篇)》为正在学习和努力掌握中级汉语语言知识和技能过程中的学生开通了一个领略中国文学艺术的渠道,打开了一扇进入中国文化殿堂的大门。

印京华
2021年6月5日

Foreword

Poetry is a form of language art that uses rhythms and rhymes to express emotions, articulate the soul, reflect life, and induce empathy. China is a country of poetry due to the unique features of its language and the long and continuous cultural history.

What are the unique features of Chinese that have made China a country of poetry? From the perspective of Chinese phonetics, there are three main unique features. First, one Chinese character has one syllable. Second, each syllable ends with a vowel or a vowel plus a nasal consonant, and there is no syllable ending with a consonant other than a nasal consonant. Third, each syllable has a tone. Naturally, the first feature makes Chinese easy to be rhythmic; the second feature makes Chinese not only sound louder but also easier to rhyme; and the third feature makes Chinese relatively more musical. These unique features of the Chinese have become handy tools for Chinese poets.

How is China as a country of poetry related to China's long and continuous cultural history? As early as 2,500 years ago, Confucius (551–479 BC), the earliest respected educator in China, used the *Classics of Poetry*, which was compiled from poems composed by imperial nobles, literati, and ordinary people in 500 years prior to his time, as a teaching material to teach his students. Since then, Chinese poetry has continued to develop along with the progress of Chinese history. Lyrics of the

Chu State, poetic expositions of the Han Dynasty, ballads of the Han Dynasty, poetry of the Tang Dynasty, ci poetry of the Song Dynasty, verses in northern tunes of the Yuan Dynasty, etc., have each become the iconic genres of the development of Chinese ancient poetry in various important historical periods and have been passed down to this day. Among them, Tang poetry is the most typical. The Tang Dynasty of China (618-907 AD) continued the civil service examinations for selecting talented young people to help emperors manage the country. The ability to write poetry became an important assessment item in the civil service examinations. In addition to the existing archaic poetry genre, the modern poetry genre, such as quatrains and regulated verses, which have strict requirements on tonal and rhyming patterns, came into being at that time. About 800 years later, in the *Complete Tang Poems*, which was compiled in 1705, more than 48,900 poems written by more than 2,300 Tang poets were included. The content covers all aspects of people's life. There is no country or historical era in human history that can produce so many poets nor so many poems. Poems of both archaic genre and modern genre can be generally referred to as ancient poems as they were written a long long time ago. Because of their catchy, beauty, wisdom, and enthusiasm, in contemporary China, they are cited by all men, women, and children. Almost everyone can blurt out or chant a few sentences of them. Poetry has been deeply integrated into the spiritual and cultural life of Chinese people.

  For students from other countries and cultures, it is necessary to experience Chinese culture and understand the taste of Chinese people. Learning, understanding, reciting, and appreciating ancient Chinese poems can be an interesting and powerful way. Ms. Ding Li carefully compiled this book, *Appreciation of Ancient Chinese Poems (Intermediate)*, based on her knowledge of Chinese poetry and her practical experience in teaching Chinese as a foreign language. Rich in content and orderly in its layout, the book has 15 lessons in all, and each lesson uses one word as a title to mark the theme of the lesson succinctly. Each lesson contains a selected ancient poem with five-character lines according to the theme, along with a brief background of the poet's creation of the poem. In order to facilitate students' recitation, each poem with five-character lines is marked with Chinese pinyin. In order to help students to experience and appreciate the poem, each poem is provided with an English translation of Mr. Xu Yuanchong and an illustration made by Ms. Wang Zongxiang. In order to ensure that students understand the poem, each lesson has a bilingual retelling of the poem in modern Chinese and English line by line, and a vocabulary list is also provided based on the new words that appear in the poem. For some general knowledge about ancient poems, each lesson has a key introduction. Each lesson in the book contains both an explanation of the poetic flavor of ancient poems, as well as simple exercises on the format of the poem and discussions on topics related to the content of the poem. At the end of each lesson, as an extension of reading, three poems, including those with five-character or seven-character lines or ci poems related to the theme of each lesson, are also selected for students to read and appreciate.

Appreciation of Chinese Ancient Poems (Intermediate) opens a channel to appreciate Chinese literature for students in the process of learning and trying to master Chinese language knowledge and skills at the intermediate level, and it also opens a door for them to enter the palace of Chinese culture.

Yin Jinghua
June 5, 2021

第一课　梅　梅　花　王安石 / 1

第二课　春　春　晓　孟浩然 / 6

第三课　江　宿建德江　孟浩然 / 12

第四课　鸟　鸟鸣涧　王　维 / 18

第五课　送　送灵澈上人　刘长卿 / 23

第六课　剑　剑　客　贾　岛 / 29

第七课　乡　杂诗三首（其二）　王　维 / 35

第八课　愁　秋浦歌（其十五）　李　白 / 41

第九课　客　问刘十九　白居易 / 47

第十课　母　游子吟　孟　郊 / 53

第十一课　望　望　岳　杜　甫 / 60

第十二课　雨　春夜喜雨　杜　甫 / 67

第十三课　山　山居秋暝　王　维 / 74

第十四课　题　题破山寺后禅院　常　建 / 80

第十五课　别　送杜少府之任蜀州　王　勃 / 86

汉英对照词汇表 / 93

诗人索引 / 99

第一课 梅

梅 花

创作背景

北宋宋神宗年间(公元1067—1085年),作为宰相的王安石(公元1021—1086年)在北宋艰难的情况下主张进行改革,但得不到支持。这首诗是王安石被罢免宰相之后,回到钟山(现在的南京紫金山)写的。

Background

Wang Anshi (1021-1086 AD), once the chief councilor during the reign of Emperor Shenzong (1067-1085 AD) in the Northern Song Dynasty, initiated a series of reforms, but received strong resistance. This poem was written by Wang Anshi when he returned to Zhongshan Mountain (now the Zijin Mountain in Nanjing) after being deposed.

梅 花

王安石

墙角数枝梅，
凌寒独自开。
遥知不是雪，
为有暗香来。

MUME BLOSSOMS

Wang Anshi

At the wall corner mume trees grow;
Against the cold they bloom apart.
How could we know they are not snow?
For fragrance unseen they impart.

（许渊冲译；Translated by Xu Yuanchong）

méi huā
梅 花

wáng ān shí
王 安 石

qiáng jiǎo shù zhī méi
墙 角 数 枝 梅，
líng hán dú zì kāi
凌 寒 独 自 开。
yáo zhī bú shì xuě
遥 知 不 是 雪，
wèi yǒu àn xiāng lái
为 有 暗 香 来。

释义

在墙角有几枝梅花,冒着寒冷的天气独自开放。我远远地就知道那不是雪了,因为有一股淡淡的香味飘来。

Paraphrase

A few mume blossoms at the corner of the wall bloom alone in the cold weather. I know they are not snow from far away, for a delicate fragrance comes with the breeze.

生词

1. 梅花:梅树的花, mume blossoms。
2. 墙角:两面墙互相接触的地方, corner formed by two walls。
3. 数:几, several, a few。
4. 枝:量词, measure word for flowers with stems intact。
5. 凌:冒着, to face defiantly。
6. 遥:遥远,很远, distant, far away。
7. 为:因为, because。
8. 暗香:淡淡的香味, a delicate fragrance。

古诗小知识

古诗意象

意象,"意"指的是诗人表达的思想和情感等,"象"表示客观形象。诗人把思想或情感等放在某个事物上,这个事物就成了意象。你觉得《梅花》这首诗的主要意象是什么?说说你的理由。

Poetry Tips

Image(Yi Xiang)

Image is expressed as "Yi Xiang" in Chinese. "Yi" relates to the thoughts or feelings expressed by the poet, and "Xiang" refers to the objective image. The poet rests his thoughts or feelings on an object, which becomes an image. What do you think is the main image in the poem *Mume Blossoms*? State your reasons.

练习题

1. 填空。

《梅花》由(　　)句组成,每句(　　)个字,全诗一共(　　)个字。第(　　)句和第(　　)句押韵。

2. 中国人喜欢梅花,并且常在古诗中赞美梅花。采访几个中国人,问问他们对梅花的印象,并根据采访谈谈你对梅花含义的理解。

3. 梅花在你的国家有特殊的含义吗?谈谈你的国家对梅花的评价。

拓展阅读

méi huā (qí sān)
梅 花(其三)

wáng miǎn
王 冕

shí yuè shuāng fēng hán
十 月 霜 风 寒,

shān mù jù cuī zhé
山 木 俱 摧 折。

独此冰玉姿,
照影清溪月。

墨　梅
王　冕

我家洗砚池头树,
朵朵花开淡墨痕。
不要人夸颜色好,
只留清气满乾坤。

白　梅
王　冕

冰雪林中著此身,
不同桃李混芳尘。
忽然一夜清香发,
散作乾坤万里春。

第二课 春

春 晓

创作背景

盛唐时期(约公元650—755年)的诗人孟浩然(公元689—740年)早年曾居住在湖北,后来想从政,但没能获得官职。《春晓》一说是孟浩然早年在湖北鹿门山隐居时写的,也有说是他晚年生病的时候写的。

Background

Meng Haoran (689-740 AD), a poet during the golden time of the Tang Dynasty (650-755 AD), lived in Hubei Province in his early years and later tried to engage in politics, but failed to get an official position. It is said that *Spring Morning* was written when he lived as a hermit in Lumen Mountain, Hubei Province in his early years. But there are some people who believe that this poem was written during his sickness in his later years.

春　晓

孟浩然

春眠不觉晓，
处处闻啼鸟。
夜来风雨声，
花落知多少。

SPRING MORNING

Meng Haoran

This spring morning in bed I'm lying,
Not to awake till birds are crying.
After one night of wind and showers,
How many are the fallen flowers!

（许渊冲译；Translated by Xu Yuanchong）

春　晓

mèng hào rán
孟　浩　然

chūn mián bù jué xiǎo
春 眠 不 觉 晓，
chù chù wén tí niǎo
处 处 闻 啼 鸟。
yè lái fēng yǔ shēng
夜 来 风 雨 声，
huā luò zhī duō shǎo
花 落 知 多 少。

❖ 释义

在春天的早上醒来,不知不觉天已经大亮,(我)听见到处都有鸟叫声。昨天晚上听到风声和雨声,不知道多少花落了?

❖ Paraphrase

Sleeping in spring morning, unaware of the dawn, I hear birds singing everywhere. Last night, the sound of wind and rain, I wonder how many flowers have fallen?

❖ 生词

1. 晓:天刚亮的时候, dawn, daybreak。
2. 眠:睡觉, to sleep。
3. 处处:到处, everywhere。
4. 闻:听见, to hear。
5. 啼:叫,(of certain birds and animals)to sing, to twitter。
6. 夜来:昨夜,昨天晚上, last night。

古诗小知识

倒　叙

倒叙是把后来发生的事情(如结果)写在前面,把先发生的事情(如原因)写在后面。倒叙的类型有三种:一是把结果提前,二是把过程中精彩的部分提前,三是由眼前事物引起回忆。《春晓》一诗从第三句开始叙述昨夜的风雨声,然后关心起落了多少花。

❖ Poetry Tips

Flashback

A flashback is used when the event that happens later (such as the outcome) comes first while the event that happens first (such as the cause) comes later. There are three types of flashbacks: first, to present the outcome first; second, to bring forward the exciting part of the process ahead; third, things in sight trigger memories of the past. *Spring Morning* describes the sound of the wind and rain last night from the third line, which triggers the author's sentimental feeling toward those fallen flowers.

1. 韵律填空。

《春晓》第( )、( )和( )句押韵。这三句的最后一个字分别是( )、( )和( ),它们的共同韵母为( )。

2. 你的国家有春天吗？春天的时候有哪些风俗习惯？

3. 你还知道哪些跟"春"有关的诗？对比这些诗与《春晓》的共同之处和不同之处。

拓展阅读

春夜喜雨
杜甫

好雨知时节,
当春乃发生。
随风潜入夜,
润物细无声。
野径云俱黑,
江船火独明。
晓看红湿处,
花重锦官城。

春日
朱熹

胜日寻芳泗水滨,
无边光景一时新。
等闲识得东风面,
万紫千红总是春。

黄鹤楼送孟浩然之广陵

李白

故人西辞黄鹤楼，
烟花三月下扬州。
孤帆远影碧空尽，
唯见长江天际流。

第三课 江

宿建德江

创作背景

唐代诗人孟浩然(公元689—740年)没能留在京城长安做官,于是无奈之下,游览山水。《宿建德江》是孟浩然在浙江建德游览时写的。

Background

Meng Haoran (689-740 AD) diverted his passion to sightseeing since his failure in pursuit of official career in Chang'an, the capital of the Tang Dynasty. *Mooring on the River at Jiande* was written when he visited Jiande, Zhejiang Province.

宿建德江

孟浩然

移舟泊烟渚，
日暮客愁新。
野旷天低树，
江清月近人。

MOORING ON THE RIVER AT JIANDE

Meng Haoran

My boat is moored near an isle in mist grey;
I'm grieved anew to see the parting day.
On boundless plain trees seem to scrape the sky;
In water clear the moon appears so nigh.

（许渊冲 译；Translated by Xu Yuanchong）

sù jiàn dé jiāng
宿 建 德 江

mèng hào rán
孟 浩 然

yí zhōu bó yān zhǔ
移 舟 泊 烟 渚，
rì mù kè chóu xīn
日 暮 客 愁 新。
yě kuàng tiān dī shù
野 旷 天 低 树，
jiāng qīng yuè jìn rén
江 清 月 近 人。

释义

把船停在烟雾笼罩的小洲边上,太阳落山增添了游子的烦恼。旷野没有边际,天空比树还低,江水清澈,月亮和人更近了。

Paraphrase

Mooring the boat towards a misty islet, with the setting sun, the traveler's sorrows grow. Wilds so vast, the sky hangs lower than the treetops. The river is so clear, making the moon close.

生词

1. 宿:住宿,过夜, to stay overnight。
2. 建德江:新安江经过浙江建德市的一段江水。
3. 移:移动,划, to move, to paddle。
4. 舟:船, boat。
5. 泊:停, to moor。
6. 烟渚:被雾笼罩的水中陆地。

 烟:雾, mist。

 渚:水中的小块陆地, islet。

7. 日暮:傍晚,太阳快落山的时候, nightfall, dusk。
8. 愁:担心,伤心, worry, sadness。
9. 野:旷野,野外, wilderness, open country, field。
10. 旷:广阔, vast, spacious。

古诗小知识

押 韵

《梅花》中"开"和"来"的韵母都是 ai,《春晓》中"鸟"和"少"都有 ao。相同韵母的字在相同位置上出现就是押韵。但古代诗韵和现代普通话并不完全一致,这也是用普通话读《宿建德江》中"新"和"人"不押韵的原因。

Poetry Tips

Rhyme

A rhyme is a repetition of similar sounds (usually, exactly the same sound) in the final words of different lines in a poem. In *Mume Blossoms*, "开" (kai) rhymes with "来" (lai), both of which end with "ai". In *Spring Morning*, "鸟" (niao) and "少" (shao) both end with "ao". A rhyme occurs when the last words in two or more lines end with the same sound. However, the rhyming in the ancient poetry are not completely consistent with that of modern poetry, which is why the words "新" and "人" in this poem do not rhyme in mandarin.

练习题

1. 请在汉语方言发音字典网站(http://cn.voicedic.com)查一查"新"和"人"在粤语或闽南语中的发音,听听它们是否押韵。

2. 诗人为什么要写"天低树"和"月近人"？谈谈你对这个问题的看法。

3. 诗人写"月近人",认为月亮跟人亲近,有一首中文歌叫《月亮代表我的心》,也是通过月亮表达感受。你对此的理解是什么?

拓展阅读

惠崇春江晚景

苏轼

竹外桃花三两枝,
春江水暖鸭先知。
蒌蒿满地芦芽短,
正是河豚欲上时。

早发白帝城

李白

朝辞白帝彩云间，
千里江陵一日还。
两岸猿声啼不住，
轻舟已过万重山。

暮江吟

白居易

一道残阳铺水中，
半江瑟瑟半江红。
可怜九月初三夜，
露似真珠月似弓。

第四课 鸟

鸟鸣涧

创作背景

《鸟鸣涧》是王维（公元701—761年）在盛唐时期游览江南时写的。当时王维住在朋友皇甫岳家中，一共写了五首诗，即《皇甫岳云溪杂题》，描写了云溪的五处风景。

Background

The Dale of Singing Birds was written by Wang Wei (701-761 AD) during his visit to the south of the Yangtze River. At that time, Wang Wei lived at Huangfu Yue's home. He wrote five poems describing the scenery of five places in Yunxi and *The Dale of Singing Birds* was one of them.

鸟鸣涧

王　维

人闲桂花落,
夜静春山空。
月出惊山鸟,
时鸣春涧中。

THE DALE OF SINGING BIRDS

Wang Wei

Sweet laurel blooms fall unenjoyed;

Vague hills dissolve into night void.

The moonrise startles birds to sing;

Their twitter fills the dale with spring.

（许渊冲译；Translated by Xu Yuanchong）

辅助理解

niǎo míng jiàn
鸟　鸣　涧
wáng　wéi
王　维

rén xián guì huā luò
人 闲 桂 花 落,
yè jìng chūn shān kōng
夜 静 春 山 空。
yuè chū jīng shān niǎo
月 出 惊 山 鸟,
shí míng chūn jiàn zhōng
时 鸣 春 涧 中。

◈ 释义

春夜安静无声,四处无人,桂花飘落,安静的夜晚更让人觉得山谷空旷。月亮出来了,山鸟被惊动,鸣叫声时而从山间的流水中传来。

◈ Paraphrase

Free and at peace, the osmanthus shed its bloom. Quiet night makes the spring mountain seems emptier. When the moon rises and the birds are roused, they sing at times in the spring stream.

◈ 生词

1. 涧:两座山之间的溪水,creek,ravine。
2. 桂花:osmanthus flowers。
3. 惊:惊动,to startle。
4. 时:时而,every now and then,at times。

古诗小知识

韵　脚

在古诗中相同位置上重复出现的同韵母字,称为韵脚。诗人写诗从韵书中选择韵脚。在韵书出现之前,诗人主要根据当时口语中的近似音选择韵脚。

◈ Poetry Tips

The Rhyming Words

In ancient poetry, the words ending with the same sound in the same position of different lines are called the rhyming words. When writing a poem, a poet chooses a rhyme from rhyme books. Before the appearance of rhyme books, a poet chooses a rhyme mainly based on the approximant sounds in spoken language at that time.

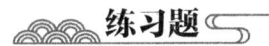 **练习题**

1. 填空。

《鸟鸣涧》第（　　）句和第（　　）句押韵,韵脚分别是（　　）和（　　）。

2. 《春晓》中也出现了"鸟"和"落花"两个意象,分析和对比这两个意象在《春晓》和《鸟鸣涧》的作用。

3. 鸟鸣涧这个地方安静吗？谈谈你对这个问题的看法。

 **拓展阅读**

滁州西涧

韦应物

独怜幽草涧边生，
上有黄鹂深树鸣。
春潮带雨晚来急，
野渡无人舟自横。

绝 句

杜 甫

两个黄鹂鸣翠柳,
一行白鹭上青天。
窗含西岭千秋雪,
门泊东吴万里船。

画眉鸟

欧阳修

百啭千声随意移,
山花红紫树高低。
始知锁向金笼听,
不及林间自在啼。

第五课 送

送灵澈上人

创作背景

唐代诗人刘长卿（公元718—790年）曾被降官职，从贬谪地回来后事业也不如意。这首诗写于刘长卿送僧人灵澈上人回竹林寺的途中。

Background

Liu Zhangqing (718-790 AD), a poet in the Tang Dynasty, was once demoted to a lower position. His political career did not go well when he returned from the place of exile. This poem was written when he was seeing the Master Ling Che off to the Zhulin Temple.

送灵澈上人

　　刘长卿

苍苍竹林寺，
杳杳钟声晚。
荷笠带斜阳，
青山独归远。

SEEING OFF A RECLUSE

　　Liu Zhangqing

To the green temple'mid bamboos
When evening bell rings, a recluse
Goes back alone. While sunset fills
His hat, he's lost in the blue hills.

（许渊冲译；Translated by Xu Yuanchong）

辅助理解

sòng líng chè shàng rén
送 灵 澈 上 人

liú zhǎng qīng
刘 长 卿

cāng cāng zhú lín sì
苍 苍 竹 林 寺，
yǎo yǎo zhōng shēng wǎn
杳 杳 钟 声 晚。
hè lì dài xié yáng
荷 笠 带 斜 阳，
qīng shān dú guī yuǎn
青 山 独 归 远。

🏵 释义

从苍翠的竹林寺里,传来低沉的晚钟。背着斗笠披着夕阳,独自回到青山,渐行渐远。

🏵 Paraphrase

From the temple amid green bamboos, comes the low sound of an evening bell. With a conical hat on his back, carrying the sunset, he goes back alone. Farther and farther down the green mountain.

🏵 生词

1. 灵澈上人:唐代著名的诗僧。

   上人:对和尚的尊称, an honorific form for Buddhist monk。

2. 苍苍:深绿, lush and green。

3. 杳杳:低沉, deep and somber。

4. 钟:用于计算时间的器具, bell。

5. 荷:背, to carry on one's shoulder or back。

6. 笠:用竹叶或草做的帽子,可以遮挡阳光和雨, bamboo or straw hat with a conical crown and broad brim, to shelter one from the sun and rain。

7. 斜阳:傍晚时西斜的太阳,夕阳, setting sun。

8. 青山:长满绿色植物的山, green mountain。

9. 归:返回, to go back to。

古诗小知识

借景抒情

借景抒情指的是诗人不直接表达情感,而是通过写景把情感融入景物之中,委婉地表达出来。《送灵澈上人》一诗从颜色和声音入手,用"苍苍""杳杳"描写青山、竹林和寺庙,营造出深远的氛围,表达诗人送别灵澈上人的深情。

Poetry Tips

Expressing Emotions by Describing the Scenery

Expressing emotions by describing the scenery indicates that the poet does not express his emotions directly, but in a euphemistic way by integrating them into the scenery description. *Seeing off a Recluse* starts with the description of color and sound, and uses the words "苍苍" and "杳杳" to describe the green mountains, bamboo forest and the temple, thus creating a profound atmosphere and expressing the poet's reluctance to say farewell to Master Ling Che.

练习题

1. 填空。

《送灵澈上人》的第(　　)句和第(　　)句押韵,韵脚分别是(　　)和(　　),共同的韵母是(　　)。

2. 诗人送别灵澈上人的时间是什么时候?从诗中找出线索,谈谈你对这个问题的看法。

3. 谈谈你的送别经历(提示:人物、时间、地点、心情等)。

 拓展阅读

山中送别
王维

山中相送罢，
日暮掩柴扉。
春草明年绿，
王孙归不归？

渡荆门送别
李白

渡远荆门外，
来从楚国游。
山随平野尽，
江入大荒流。
月下飞天镜，
云生结海楼。
仍怜故乡水，
万里送行舟。

sòng yǒu rén
送友人

lǐ bái
李白

qīng shān héng běi guō
青山横北郭，
bái shuǐ rào dōng chéng
白水绕东城。
cǐ dì yī wéi bié
此地一为别，
gū péng wàn lǐ zhēng
孤蓬万里征。
fú yún yóu zǐ yì
浮云游子意，
luò rì gù rén qíng
落日故人情。
huī shǒu zì zī qù
挥手自兹去，
xiāo xiāo bān mǎ míng
萧萧班马鸣。

第六课 剑

剑 客

创作背景

唐代诗人贾岛（公元779—843年）在别人的劝说下参加科举考试。他认为凭自己的才学一定能考中，不把考试放在眼里。结果他却没能考上。贾岛认为是自己在考试中写的诗得罪了一些人，无可奈何之下写了这首诗。

Background

Jia Dao (779-843 AD), a poet in the Tang Dynasty, was persuaded to take the imperial civil examination. He thought that with his talent and knowledge, he was bound to be successful, so he didn't take the examination seriously. As a result, he failed. Jia Dao thought his failure was caused by the poem he wrote in the examination, which offended some people in authority. Under this circumstance did he write this poem to express his desperation and hopelessness.

剑 客

贾 岛

十年磨一剑，
霜刃未曾试。
今日把示君，
谁有不平事？

A SWORDSMAN

Jia Dao

I've sharpened my sword for ten years;
I do not know if it will pierce.
I show its blade to you today.
O who has any grievance? Say!

（许渊冲译；Translated by Xu Yuanchong）

 辅助理解

jiàn　　kè
剑　　客

jiǎ　dǎo
贾 岛

shí nián mó yí jiàn
十 年 磨 一 剑，
shuāng rèn wèi céng shì
霜 刃 未 曾 试。
jīn rì bǎ shì jūn
今 日 把 示 君，
shuí yǒu bù píng shì
谁 有 不 平 事？

释义

十年磨出一把剑,剑刃锋利,还没试过。今天把它拿给您看看,谁有不平之事?

Paraphrase

It has taken me ten years to grind the sword. Its frosty edges have not been tested yet. Today I'm showing this sword to you. Is there anyone who has a grievance?

生词

1. 剑:一种细长的武器,两边有刃,long sword with double-edged blade。
2. 客:这里指对从事某种活动的人的称呼,person engaged in some particular pursuit。
3. 磨:使东西光滑或锋利,to polish, to grind。
4. 霜:像霜一样的白色,white hoar。
5. 刃:刀或剑上锋利的部分,edges(of a knife, sword, etc.), blades。
6. 未曾:曾经没有,never before, haven't。
7. 示:把东西拿出来让人看,to show。
8. 君:用于尊称对方,您,you。
9. 不平:不公平,unfair, unjust。

古诗小知识

古诗表现手法——托物言志

诗人通过描写客观事物的某个特点来表达某种感情、思想和志向等。这些事物的主要特点和诗人本身有相似点。第一课《梅花》中,诗人王安石写的是梅,说的是人,既可以理解成他说的是自己的品德,也可以理解成他希望自己能成为有这种品德的人。

Poetry Tips

Expressing Ambitions by Describing Concrete Objects

Expressing ambitions by describing concrete objects indicates that a poet expresses his feelings, thoughts, ambitions, etc., by describing a certain character of concrete objects. The main character of these things is similar to that of the poet himself. In Lesson One *Mume Blossoms*, what Wang Anshi wrote is about mume blossoms while what he meant is about human character. It can be understood that he was talking about his own moral character, or that he hoped he could become a person with such moral character.

练习题

1. 填空。

《剑客》第( )句和第( )句押韵,韵脚分别是( )和( ),共同的韵母是( )。

2. "剑"在你们国家的文化中一般有什么含义？对比你们文化中的含义和贾岛《剑客》诗中的含义。

3. 中国有句谚语叫"路见不平,拔刀相助",谈谈你对这句谚语的理解。

 拓展阅读

李都尉古剑

白居易

古剑寒黯黯,
铸来几千秋。
白光纳日月,
紫气排斗牛。
有客借一观,
爱之不敢求。
湛然玉匣中,
秋水澄不流。
至宝有本性,
精刚无与俦。
可使寸寸折,
不能绕指柔。
愿快直士心,
将断佞臣头。
不愿报小怨,
夜半刺私仇。
劝君慎所用,
无作神兵羞。

咏宝剑

崔融

宝剑出昆吾,
龟龙夹采珠。
五精初献术,
千户竞沦都。
匣气冲牛斗,
山形转辘轳。
欲知天下贵,
持此问风胡。

送郑少府入辽共赋侠客远从戎

骆宾王

边烽警榆塞,
侠客度桑乾。
柳叶开银镝,
桃花照玉鞍。
满月临弓影,
连星入剑端。
不学燕丹客,
徒歌易水寒。

第七课 乡

杂诗三首（其二）

创作背景

关于这首诗的背景主要有两种说法。一种是唐代诗人王维（公元701—761年）在年轻的时候所写，因为他十五岁就离开家乡到长安准备科举考试了。另一种说法是王维做官已经很久了，遇到从家乡来的人，于是写了这首诗。

Background

There are two versions about the background of this poem. One goes like this: it was written by Wang Wei (701–761 AD), a poet in the Tang Dynasty, when he was a young man. At the age of fifteen, he left his hometown for Chang'an to prepare for the imperial civil examination. Another version is that Wang Wei, who had been an official and left his hometown for a long time, wrote this poem when he met a visitor from his hometown.

杂诗三首（其二）

王 维

君自故乡来，
应知故乡事。
来日绮窗前，
寒梅著花未？

OUR NATIVE PLACE

Wang Wei

You come from native place;
What happened there you'd know.
Did mume blossoms in face
Of my gauze window blow?

（许渊冲译；Translated by Xu Yuanchong）

辅助理解

zá shī sān shǒu qí èr
杂诗三首（其二）

wáng wéi
王 维

jūn zì gù xiāng lái
君自故乡来，
yīng zhī gù xiāng shì
应知故乡事。
lái rì qǐ chuāng qián
来日绮窗前，
hán méi zhuó huā wèi
寒梅著花未？

释义

您是刚从我家乡来的,一定了解家乡的事情。请问您来的时候,我家窗户前那棵寒梅开花了没有?

Paraphrase

Since you have come from our hometown, you should know what's happening there. By the window the day you left, were the winter plums in bloom?

生词

1. 杂诗:不定题目的诗,跟"无题诗"类似,主题广泛,similar to the poems without titles but with a wide range of subjects。

2. 故乡:出生地或住过很长时间的地方,家乡,hometown, native place, birthplace。

3. 来日:来的时候,past days。

4. 绮窗:精美的窗户,beautifully decorated window。

5. 寒梅:梅花,因为在天气寒冷的时候开花,所以也叫寒梅,plum blossoms。

6. 著花未:开没开花?

著花:开花, to blossom。

未:用在问句句末,表示疑问,(used at the end of questions, indicating doubt) or not。

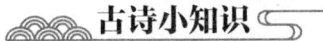 古诗小知识

白　描

白描是中国国画的一种表现形式,指的是只用墨线勾画事物,后来也被古诗评论采用,作为叙事和描写的一种手法。其特点为简洁清晰,不加修饰。《杂诗(其二)》中诗人通过向同乡询问家乡的情况,表达自己对家乡的思念。

Poetry Tips

Line Drawing

Line drawing, a technique used in Chinese painting, refers to outline objects with only ink lines. Later, it was also adopted by ancient poetry critics as a way of narration and description. Line drawing is featured with concise, simple, straight forward style of writing, with no additional decoration. In *Our Native Place,* the poet expressed his homesickness by asking a fellow townsman about what happened in his hometown and at his home.

练习题

1. 请在汉语方言发音字典网站(http://cn.voicedic.com)查一查"事"和"未"在粤语或闽南语中的发音,听听这两个字是否押韵。

2. 为什么诗人一见到同乡就问梅花开没开?请谈谈你对这个问题的理解。

3. 如果你已经离开故乡很长时间,在外地遇到了从故乡来的人,你会问什么问题?

拓展阅读

杂诗三首(其一)
王维

家住孟津河,
门对孟津口。
常有江南船,
寄书家中否?

杂诗三首(其三)
王维

已见寒梅发,
复闻啼鸟声。
心心视春草,
畏向玉阶生。

回乡偶书

贺知章

少小离家老大回，
乡音无改鬓毛衰。
儿童相见不相识，
笑问客从何处来。

第八课 愁

秋浦歌(其十五)

创作背景

唐代诗人李白(公元701—762年)在游览秋浦的时候,创作了组诗《秋浦歌》,共十七首,这是第十五首。当时,五十多岁的李白已经离开长安将近十年,却仍然找不到机会实现自己的政治理想。

Background

During his visit to Qiupu, Li Bai (701-762 AD) composed a series of seventeen poems called *Song of Qiupu*. This was the fifteenth. When he wrote this poem, Li Bai was already in his fifties and away from Chang'an for nearly a decade, but he still could not find an opportunity to realize his political ambitions.

秋浦歌(其十五)

李 白

白发三千丈，
缘愁似个长。
不知明镜里，
何处得秋霜？

MY WHITE HAIR

Li Bai

Long, long is my lightening hair;
Long, long is it laden with care.
I look into my mirror bright;
From where comes autumn frost so white?

（许渊冲译；Translated by Xu Yuanchong）

辅助理解

qiū pǔ gē　qí shí wǔ
秋 浦 歌(其 十 五)

lǐ　bái
李　白

bái fà sān qiān zhàng
白 发 三 千 丈，
yuán chóu sì gè cháng
缘 愁 似 个 长。
bù zhī míng jìng lǐ
不 知 明 镜 里，
hé chù dé qiū shuāng
何 处 得 秋 霜？

🏶 释义

（我的）白头发有三千丈,因为我有像这样长的忧愁。不知道明亮镜子里的我,哪里得来这秋霜一样的白发?

🏶 **Paraphrase**

My hoary hair grows miles long, because my sorrows are as long. Looking into the bright and clear mirror, I feel lost, how autumn frost gets in there!

🏶 生词

1. 秋浦:地名,在安徽省池州市。
2. 三千丈:形容很长,extremely long。
丈:长度单位,1丈大概等于3.3米,a Chinese unit of length, equal to 3⅓ meters。
3. 缘:因为,because, for (reason)。
4. 似:像,to be similar。
5. 个:这样,this。
6. 明镜:明亮的镜子,也指河水,bright mirror, which indicates that the river is like a bright mirror。
7. 得:取得,获得,to get。
8. 秋霜:指白发。形容头发白得像秋天的霜,autumn frost, which refers to white hair here。

古诗小知识

诗 眼

诗眼是诗歌评论中的术语。诗中的某个字用得简练或生动,会提升整句诗的艺术表现力。诗歌评论家将诗中用得简练生动的字称为"诗眼"。《秋浦歌(其十五)》的诗眼是"何处得秋霜"的"得"。

Poetry Tips

Poetic Eye

Poetry eye is a term used in poetry criticism. If a word in the poem is expressive and vivid enough and enhances the artistic effect of the whole poem, it is called "poetic eye" by critics. The poetic eye of *My White Hair* is the "得" in the line "何处得秋霜".

练习题

1. 《秋浦歌（其十五）》的韵脚是哪些？押的是哪个韵？

2. 诗人的白发真的有三千丈那么长吗？诗人为什么这样写？请谈谈你对这两个问题的理解。

3. 有句歇后语叫"伍子胥过昭关——一夜愁白了头"。春秋时期，伍子胥被追杀，他一连几夜愁得睡不着觉，连头发也愁白了。伍子胥头发变白后，没有被认出来，便成功从昭关逃跑。你们国家有通过身体等的变化表达"愁"的说法吗？

 **拓展阅读**

登幽州台歌

陈子昂

前不见古人,
后不见来者。
念天地之悠悠,
独怆然而涕下!

宣州谢朓楼饯别校书叔云

李白

弃我去者,
昨日之日不可留;
乱我心者,
今日之日多烦忧。
长风万里送秋雁,
对此可以酣高楼。
蓬莱文章建安骨,
中间小谢又清发。
俱怀逸兴壮思飞,
欲上青天览明月。

抽刀断水水更流，
举杯消愁愁更愁。
人生在世不称意，
明朝散发弄扁舟。

虞美人

李煜

春花秋月何时了？
往事知多少。
小楼昨夜又东风，
故国不堪回首月明中。
雕栏玉砌应犹在，
只是朱颜改。
问君能有几多愁？
恰似一江春水向东流。

第九课 客

问刘十九

创作背景

这是一首关于邀请朋友喝酒的诗,是唐代诗人白居易(公元772—846年)在江州(江西省九江市)做官期间写的。刘十九是白居易在江州的朋友,"十九"指的是他在家中的排行。

Background

This is a poem about inviting a friend for a drink. It was written by Bai Juyi (772-846 AD) when he was an official in Jiangzhou (now Jiujiang, Jiangxi Province). Liu Shijiu was Bai's friend in Jiangzhou. "Shijiu" in Chinese means "nineteen", which indicates Liu is the nineteenth child in the family.

问刘十九

白居易

绿蚁新醅酒，
红泥小火炉。
晚来天欲雪，
能饮一杯无？

AN INVITATION

Bai Juyi

My new brew gives green glow;
My red clay stove flames up.
At dusk it threatens snow.
Won't you come for a cup?

（许渊冲译；Translated by Xu Yuanchong）

辅助理解

wèn liú shí jiǔ
问 刘 十 九
bái jū yì
白 居 易

lù yǐ xīn pēi jiǔ
绿 蚁 新 醅 酒，
hóng ní xiǎo huǒ lú
红 泥 小 火 炉。
wǎn lái tiān yù xuě
晚 来 天 欲 雪，
néng yǐn yì bēi wú
能 饮 一 杯 无？

第九课 客

释义

新酿的、还没过滤的酒上浮着绿色的泡沫,它正暖在红泥做的小火炉上。天色已晚,而且又将下一场雪,你能来跟我喝一杯吗?

Paraphrase

There is a gleam of green in the new wine, being heated on the red-clay stove. It's getting dark and going to snow. What about having a cup of wine?

生词

1. 绿蚁:新酿的米酒还没过滤时,酒面浮起浅绿色的泡沫,和蚂蚁一样细小,所以叫"绿蚁", green ants。

2. 醅:没有过滤的酒, unfiltered wine。

3. 泥:土和水混合成的东西, mud, clay。

4. 火炉:用来取暖和做饭的炉子, heating stove。

5. 晚来:傍晚, night fall。

6. 欲:将要, about to, going to。

7. 无:表示疑问, question word for yes-no questions。

古诗小知识

新醅酒

"醅"指的是没有过滤的酒,喝之前需要过滤。"绿蚁新醅酒"指的是新酿的酒,酒渣还没有完全过滤掉,有一层细小的浅绿色泡沫。在唐代,人们喝酒讲究温热了再喝。因此,到了寒冷的冬天,往往在小火炉上温一壶酒。

Poetry Tips

Newly Fermented Grain Wine

Newly fermented grain wine refers to the unfiltered alcohol that needs to be filtered before drinking. "绿蚁新醅酒" means "Green bubbles—newly fermented wine", the sediments of which have not been completely filtered out and therefore, there is a layer of fine, light green foam. In the Tang Dynasty, people used to warm the wine up before they drank it. Therefore, in the cold winter, they would warm a pot of wine on a small stove.

练习题

1. 填空。

《问刘十九》第(　　)句和第(　　)句押韵,韵脚分别是(　　)和(　　),共同的韵母是(　　)。

2. 请把本诗用自己的话改写成一份邀请函。

3. 你们国家会通过哪些方式邀请朋友共享美食美酒?

约客

赵师秀

黄梅时节家家雨,
青草池塘处处蛙。
有约不来过夜半,
闲敲棋子落灯花。

客至

杜甫

舍南舍北皆春水,
但见群鸥日日来。
花径不曾缘客扫,
蓬门今始为君开。
盘飧市远无兼味,
樽酒家贫只旧醅。
肯与邻翁相对饮,
隔篱呼取尽馀杯。

过故人庄

孟浩然

故人具鸡黍,
邀我至田家。
绿树村边合,
青山郭外斜。
开轩面场圃,
把酒话桑麻。
待到重阳日,
还来就菊花。

第十课 母

游子吟

创作背景

唐代诗人孟郊（公元 751—814 年）年幼时便失去了父亲，由母亲抚养成人。孟郊五十岁时当上了溧阳县尉，结束了长年漂泊的生活，于是把母亲接来一起住。诗人在这首诗里回忆了离家之前母亲为他缝衣服的场景。

Background

Meng Jiao (751-814 AD), a poet in the Tang Dynasty, lost his father when he was young and was raised by his mother. When Meng Jiao was fifty years old, he became a sheriff in Liyang County and ended his wandering life for many years. After he settled down, he took his mother to live with him. The poem presents a mother who sews clothes for her son, worrying about his pending travel away from home.

游子吟

孟　郊

慈母手中线，
游子身上衣。
临行密密缝，
意恐迟迟归。
谁言寸草心，
报得三春晖。

SONG OF THE PARTING SON

Meng Jiao

From the threads a mother's hand weaves
A gown for parting son is made,
Sewn stitch by stitch before he leaves
For fear his return be delayed,
Such kindness as young grass receives
From the warm sun can be repaid?

（许渊冲译；Translated by Xu Yuanchong）

yóu zǐ yín
游 子 吟

mèng jiāo
孟　郊

cí mǔ shǒu zhōng xiàn
慈 母 手 中 线，
yóu zǐ shēn shàng yī
游 子 身 上 衣。

lín xíng mì mì féng
临行密密缝,
yì kǒng chí chí guī
意恐迟迟归。
shuí yán cùn cǎo xīn
谁言寸草心,
bào dé sān chūn huī
报得三春晖。

释义

慈祥的母亲用手中的针线,为远游的儿子缝制身上的衣服。即将出发之前一针一针密密地缝,是因为担心儿子如果回来得晚,衣服会破损。有谁敢说子女像小草那样渺小的孝心,能够报答像春天灿烂的阳光一样的母爱呢?

Paraphrase

A gracious mother with the thread in her hands, makes clothes for her wayward boy. She sews carefully and mends thoroughly, dreading the delays that will keep him late from home. But how much love does the inch-long grass have to repay for the light of the sun in three spring months?

生词

1. 游子:出门远游的人, person traveling or living far from home。
2. 吟:一种诗歌类型, song, a type of classical poetry。
3. 慈母:慈祥的母亲, loving, caring mother。
4. 临行:将要离开, before leaving。
   临:将要, just before, about to。
5. 密密:很细、很紧密, tight, close。
6. 缝:用针和线把东西连起来, to stitch, to sew。
7. 意恐:心里害怕,担心, to worry。
8. 寸草:小草, young grass。
9. 报:报答, to repay。
10. 三春晖:春天灿烂的阳光。

三春：旧称农历正月为孟春，二月为仲春，三月为季春，合称三春，the three spring months。

晖：阳光，sunshine。

古诗小知识

古体诗

诗从创作规则的角度可以分为古体诗和近体诗。这一分类开始于唐代。唐代形成了字数、押韵等方面都有规则的诗，唐代人称之为近体诗。而产生于唐代以前，并且不受规则限制的自由诗，唐代人称之为古体诗。唐代及其以后仍然有古体诗，后来的人继续使用唐代人对这两类诗的说法。

Poetry Tips

Ancient Poetry

In terms of writing rules, poetry can be divided into ancient poetry and modern poetry. This classification began in the Tang Dynasty. The poetry in the Tang Dynasty belongs to modern poetry, which consists of a regular number of words and rhymes. However, the free-style poetry before the Tang Dynasty is referred as ancient poetry, which is not restricted by rules. Ancient poetry still exists in the Tang Dynasty and later periods, and today we continue to use the two terms proposed by the people in the Tang Dynasty.

练习题

1. 你离开家之前，你的母亲说了什么？做了什么？《游子吟》中母亲表达爱的方式和你母亲表达爱的方式一样吗？为什么？

2. 诗人孟郊认为母爱像"三春晖",你认为母爱像什么？请谈一谈你对母爱的理解。

3. 你平时是怎么表达对母亲的感谢和爱的？母亲节那天你会怎么做？

suì mù dào jiā
岁 暮 到 家

jiǎng shì quán
蒋 士 铨

ài zǐ xīn wú jìn
爱 子 心 无 尽,
guī jiā xǐ jí chén
归 家 喜 及 辰 。

寒衣针线密，
家信墨痕新。
见面怜清瘦，
呼儿问苦辛。
低徊愧人子，
不敢叹风尘。

送母回乡

李商隐

停车茫茫顾，
困我成楚囚。
感伤从中起，
悲泪哽在喉。
慈母方病重，
欲将名医投。
车接今在急，
天竟情不留！
母爱无所报，
人生更何求！

墨萱图(其一)

王冕

灿灿萱草花,
罗生北堂下。
南风吹其心,
摇摇为谁吐?
慈母倚门情,
游子行路苦。
甘旨日以疏,
音问日以阻。
举头望云林,
愧听慧鸟语。

第十一课 望

望 岳

创作背景

二十多岁的杜甫(公元712—770年)在山东一带漫游时写下了这首诗。虽然杜甫当时没有通过进士考试,但是依旧在诗中表达了自己的雄心壮志。

Background

Du Fu (712-770 AD) wrote this poem while roaming around Shandong Province in his 20s. Although Du Fu failed the imperial examination, he expressed his ambitions in his poem.

望 岳

杜 甫

岱宗夫如何?
齐鲁青未了。

造化钟神秀,

阴阳割昏晓。

荡胸生曾云,

决眦入归鸟。

会当凌绝顶,

一览众山小。

Gazing at Mount Tai

Du Fu

O peak of peaks, how high it stands!

One boundless green overspreads two States.

A marvel done by Nature's hands,

Clouds rise there from and lave my breast;

My eyes are strained to see birds fleet,

I must ascend the mountain's crest,

It dwarfs all peaks under feet.

（许渊冲译；Translated by Xu Yuanchong）

 辅助理解

wàng yuè
望 岳

dù fǔ
杜 甫

dài zōng fú rú hé
岱 宗 夫 如 何？

qí lǔ qīng wèi liǎo
齐 鲁 青 未 了。

zào huà zhōng shén xiù
造 化 钟 神 秀,

<pre>
       yīn yáng gē hūn xiǎo
        阴 阳 割 昏 晓。
       dàng xiōng shēng céng yún
        荡 胸 生 曾 云,
       jué zì rù guī niǎo
        决 眦 入 归 鸟。
       huì dāng líng jué dǐng
        会 当 凌 绝 顶,
       yì lǎn zhòng shān xiǎo
        一 览 众 山 小。
</pre>

释义

五岳之首的泰山是怎样的啊?在齐鲁的大地上,那青翠的山色没有尽头。大自然给了这儿神奇秀丽的景色,山南和山北分割了暮色和晨光。云彩层出不穷,心胸因此开阔,极力睁大眼睛,可以看见归巢的飞鸟。一定要登上泰山的山顶,那时候俯瞰其他的山,它们看起来是多么渺小!

Paraphrase

How about the Mount Tai, the first of the Five Great Mountains? There are endless mountains in Qi and Lu. Wonders and beauties get together in these regions, dusk in the north of the hill and daybreak the south. Rotating clouds make you shiver and shake violently, opening the eyes people hurry to count returning birds. I'm determined to climb up the peaks among the hills, to see multitude of hills and know how little they are.

生词

1. 望岳:仰望泰山,杜甫写过三首望岳诗,这首诗是望东岳诗, to look up at Mount Tai。

2. 岱宗:指泰山;"岱"是泰山的别称,由于它居五岳之首,因此被称为岱宗;五岳:泰山(东岳)、衡山(南岳)、华山(西岳)、恒山(北岳)、嵩山(中岳); another name for Mount Tai as principal of the Five Great Mountains。

3. 夫如何:怎么样呢, how about。

夫：语气词，强调疑问的语气。

4. 齐鲁：春秋时期（约公元前770—前476年）的两个国家的名字；齐国位于泰山东北，鲁国位于泰山西南；现在用齐鲁代称山东；two states during Spring and Autumn Period（c. 770-476 BC）。

5. 青未了：山色没有边际，endless mountains。

未了：没有尽头。

6. 造化：指大自然，nature。

7. 钟：聚集，to concentrate。

8. 神秀：指泰山神奇秀丽的景色，magical and beautiful views。

9. 阴阳：阴这里指山的北面，阳指山的南面。*Yin* refers to the north of the mountain and *Yang* refers to the south of the mountain.

10. 割昏晓：分割成黄昏和早晨那样明显。此句是说泰山很高，在同一时间，山南山北好像早晨和晚上，明暗完全不同。It divides north from south, dusk from dawn.

昏晓：黄昏和早晨。

11. 荡胸：让心胸开阔，to broad the mind。

12. 曾：同"层"，层出不穷，to emerge in an endless stream。

13. 决眦：眼角好像要裂开，极力睁大眼睛，to keep eyes open。决：裂开；眦：眼角。

14. 入归鸟：看到归巢的鸟，saw homing birds。

入：收入眼底，即看见。归鸟：回到鸟巢的鸟。

15. 会当：一定要，must。

16. 凌绝顶：登上最高峰，to reach the highest peak。凌：登上；绝顶：山峰最高处。

古诗小知识

泰　山

泰山位于中国山东省泰安市。在中国文化中，东方是有优势的方位，而泰山由于处于东方而被尊为"五岳之首"，许多古代君王会到泰山举行封禅大典。泰山优越的地理位置和深远的历史背景，让文人墨客慕名游览，留下了许多作品。一提到写泰山的诗,人们首先想到的往往是杜甫的《望岳》。

❀ Poetry Tips

Mount Tai

Mount Tai is located in Tai'an, Shandong Province. In Chinese culture, the east is the dominant location, and Mount Tai is respected as the "First of the Five Great Mountains" because of its location in the east. For thousands of years, Mount Tai has been the sacred mountain where Emperors held the ceremony of offering sacrifices to heaven and earth to pray and show gratitude for peace and prosperity. The geographical advantage and profound historical significance of Mount Tai have attracted scholars and calligraphers in every dynasty to visit the mountain and leave many works behind. However, when it comes to poems about Mount Tai, Du Fu's *Gazing at Mount Tai* is always the first that comes into our mind.

练习题

1. 填空。

《望岳》由(　　)句组成。第(　　)句押韵,韵脚分别是(　　),共同的韵母是(　　)。

2. 你最喜欢《望岳》中的哪一句?为什么喜欢这一句?

3. 在你们国家,"山"代表什么?

拓展阅读

chūn wàng
春 望

dù fǔ
杜 甫

guó pò shān hé zài
国 破 山 河 在,
chéng chūn cǎo mù shēn
城 春 草 木 深。
gǎn shí huā jiàn lèi
感 时 花 溅 泪,
hèn bié niǎo jīng xīn
恨 别 鸟 惊 心。
fēng huǒ lián sān yuè
烽 火 连 三 月,
jiā shū dǐ wàn jīn
家 书 抵 万 金。
bái tóu sāo gèng duǎn
白 头 搔 更 短,
hún yù bú shèng zān
浑 欲 不 胜 簪。

望天门山

李白

天门中断楚江开,
碧水东流至此回。
两岸青山相对出,
孤帆一片日边来。

峨眉山月歌

李白

峨眉山月半轮秋,
影入平羌江水流。
夜发清溪向三峡,
思君不见下渝州。

第十二课 雨

春夜喜雨

创作背景

在经历流离生活和旱灾之后,杜甫来到四川成都的草堂居住,这首诗是他定居在此的第二年写的。杜甫在草堂种菜养花,过着安定的晚年生活。

Background

Du Fu settled in a cottage in Chengdu, Sichuan Province after years of wandering life and sufferings from extreme drought. This poem was written in the second year after Du Fu settled down. He grew vegetables and flowers in front of his cottage and lived a peaceful life in his later years.

春夜喜雨

杜 甫

好雨知时节，
当春乃发生。
随风潜入夜，
润物细无声。
野径云俱黑，
江船火独明。
晓看红湿处，
花重锦官城。

HAPPY RAIN ON A SPRING NIGHT

Du Fu

Good rain knows its time right;
It will fall when comes spring.
With wind it steals in night;
Mute, it moistens each thing.
O'er wild lanes dark cloud spreads;
In boat a lantern looms.
Dawn sees saturated reds;
The town's heavy with blooms.

（许渊冲译；Translated by Xu Yuanchong）

春夜喜雨

杜甫

好雨知时节，
当春乃发生。
随风潜入夜，
润物细无声。
野径云俱黑，
江船火独明。
晓看红湿处，
花重锦官城。

释义

好雨好像知道应该何时下，当春天万物生长的时候就降落下来。在夜里，细密的雨随着春风落下，无声地滋润着万物。往野外小路看去，天上的云黑茫茫一片，只有江上渔船的灯火亮着。天亮之后，再看那带着雨水的花朵更加鲜艳，成都一片繁花盛开的景象。

Paraphrase

The rain knows the time, knows it is spring and punctually comes. With the wind it came quietly at night, came softly and silently to moisten all and helped them grow. I walked down the wild road under the dark cloud, and saw the only light from the boat. In the morning I looked into the Jin city where it was red and wet, and found flowers booming everywhere.

生词

1. 乃：于是，就，so。
2. 发生：这里指下雨，to rain。
3. 潜：悄悄地，secretly, quietly, silently。
4. 润：滋养，to moisten。
5. 野径：野外的小路，track in the wilderness。
6. 俱：都，all。
7. 锦官城：也叫锦城，成都的别称，another name for Chengdu。

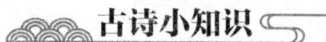古诗小知识

中国城市在古诗中的别称

城市	古诗中的别称
西安	长安
杭州	钱塘
南京	金陵
苏州	姑苏
咸阳	渭城
荆州	江陵
诸城	密州
临沂、青岛、潍坊、日照一带	琅琊

Poetry Tips

Ancient Names for Present Chinese Cities

Present Names	Ancient Names
Xi'an	Chang'an
Hangzhou	Qiantang
Nanjing	Jinling

(to be continued)

Present Names	Ancient Names
Suzhou	Gusu
Xianyang	Weicheng
Jingzhou	Jiangling
Zhucheng	Mizhou
Linyi, Qingdao, Weifang, Rizhao	Langya

练习题

1. 填空。

《春夜喜雨》由(　　)句组成，每句(　　)个字，全诗一共(　　)个字。第(　　)句、第(　　)句和第(　　)句押韵。

2. 有人认为教育是润物无声的，根据春雨的特点和你的理解，你认为"润物细无声"还可以指什么？

3. 中国有句谚语叫"春雨贵如油"。为什么春雨是宝贵的？请谈谈你对这个问题的看法。

夜雨寄北

李商隐

君问归期未有期，
巴山夜雨涨秋池。
何当共剪西窗烛，
却话巴山夜雨时。

早春呈水部张十八员外（其一）

韩愈

天街小雨润如酥，
草色遥看近却无。
最是一年春好处，
绝胜烟柳满皇都。

咸阳城西楼晚眺

许浑

一上高城万里愁，
蒹葭杨柳似汀洲。

xī yún chū qǐ rì chén gé
溪云初起日沉阁，
shān yǔ yù lái fēng mǎn lóu
山雨欲来风满楼。
niǎo xià lǜ wú qín yuàn xī
鸟下绿芜秦苑夕，
chán míng huáng yè hàn gōng qiū
蝉鸣黄叶汉宫秋。
xíng rén mò wèn dāng nián shì
行人莫问当年事，
gù guó dōng lái wèi shuǐ liú
故国东来渭水流。

第十三课 山

山居秋暝

创作背景

晚年的王维（公元701—761年）在终南山辋川别墅过着隐居的生活，写的诗多表现自然风光。这首诗就写了初秋一场新雨之后诗人的所见所闻。

Background

In his later years, Wang Wei (701-761 AD) lived a secluded life in a villa in the Zhongnan Mountain where he wrote a large quantity of poems about natural scenery. This poem described what the poet saw and heard after a fresh rain in the early autumn.

山居秋暝

王 维

空山新雨后，
天气晚来秋。

明月松间照,
清泉石上流。
竹喧归浣女,
莲动下渔舟。
随意春芳歇,
王孙自可留。

AUTUMN EVENING IN THE MOUNTAINS

Wang Wei

After fresh rain in mountains bare

Autumn permeates evening air.

Among pine-trees bright moonbeams peer;

O'er crystal stones flows water clear.

Bamboos whisper of washer-maids;

Lotus stirs when fishing boat wades.

Though fragrant spring may pass away,

Still here's the place for you to stay.

（许渊冲译；Translated by Xu Yuanchong）

shān jū qiū míng
山 居 秋 暝

wáng wéi
王 维

kōng shān xīn yǔ hòu
空 山 新 雨 后,
tiān qì wǎn lái qiū
天 气 晚 来 秋。

míng yuè sōng jiān zhào
明 月 松 间 照，
qīng quán shí shàng liú
清 泉 石 上 流。
zhú xuān guī huàn nǚ
竹 喧 归 浣 女，
lián dòng xià yú zhōu
莲 动 下 渔 舟。
suí yì chūn fāng xiē
随 意 春 芳 歇，
wáng sūn zì kě liú
王 孙 自 可 留。

释义

空旷的山经过了一场新雨的沐浴。夜晚降临，天气凉爽，仿佛已经到了秋天。明月从松树的间隙洒下月光。清澈的泉水在山石上流淌。竹林里传来声响，是洗衣的姑娘们回来了。莲叶摇动，应该是渔船从上游而来。就让春天的芳菲随意歇息吧，隐居的人在秋日的山中可以久留。

Paraphrase

Empty hills look pure as a recent rain refines, as dusk is falling autumn is felt in the bones. A silvery moon is shining through the pines. The limpid brooks are gurgling over the stones. Bamboos laugh out as girls from washing whirl. The lotus stirs where boats out fishing curl. The scents of spring may go; that's Nature's will. This season here attracts the noble still.

生词

1. 暝：天黑，dusk。
2. 喧：喧哗，大声说话，clamor。
3. 浣：洗衣服，to wash clothes。
4. 春芳：春天的花草和芳香，spring flowers。
5. 王孙：古代对贵族青年男子的尊称，这里指隐居的人，offspring of the nobility, here refers to hermit。

古诗小知识

用 典

用典是古诗中常用的一种艺术表现方法,指的是引用经典书籍、前人古诗、神话传说、历史故事等。用典主要有以下形式:一是直接引用前人的语句;二是用自己的话写出前人的语句;三是引用神话传说;四是明白地指出引用的历史故事的细节;四是引用历史故事,但是不明显地出现细节;五是反用历史故事,与引用内容的意思相反。《山居秋暝》最后一句反用了淮南小山《招隐士》"王孙兮归来,山中兮不可久留"。

Poetry Tips

Allusion

Allusion, a technique commonly used in poetry, refers to quoting from classic books, ancient poems, myths and legends, historical stories and so on. The main forms of allusion are as follows: first, to directly quote the words of the predecessors; second, to paraphrase the words of the predecessors; third, to quote myths and legends; fourth, to quote historical stories with clear and obvious details; fifth, to quote historical stories, but without clear and obvious details; sixth, to use historical stories in reverse purpose, which is contrary to the original meaning of the quoted stories. The last line in *Autumn Evening in the Mountains* quotes a sentence in *The Hermit* by Huainan Xiaoshan instead, "王孙兮归来,山中兮不可久留", which means "Come back for it is not wise to stay in the mountains for long", but Wang Wei changes its original meaning in his *Autumn Evening in the Mountains*.

练习题

1. 填空。

《山居秋暝》由(　　)句组成,每句(　　)个字,全诗一共(　　)个字。第(　　)句、第(　　)句和第(　　)句押韵。

2. 用典作为一种表现方法，有好的一方面，也有不好的一方面。你认为用典对诗歌有哪些影响？

3. 你们国家的文学作品中有用典这样的表现方法吗？

拓展阅读

lù zhài
鹿 柴

wáng wéi
王 维

kōng shān bú jiàn rén
空 山 不 见 人，
dàn wén rén yǔ xiǎng
但 闻 人 语 响。
fǎn jǐng rù shēn lín
返 景 入 深 林，
fù zhào qīng tái shàng
复 照 青 苔 上。

山居即事

王维

寂寞掩柴扉,
苍茫对落晖。
鹤巢松树遍,
人访荜门稀。
绿竹含新粉,
红莲落故衣。
渡头烟火起,
处处采菱归。

早秋山居

温庭筠

山近觉寒早,
草堂霜气晴。
树凋窗有日,
池满水无声。
果落见猿过,
叶干闻鹿行。
素琴机虑静,
空伴夜泉清。

第十四课 题

题破山寺后禅院

创作背景

唐代诗人常建(公元708—765年)仕途失意之后寄情于山水,常到山林中游览。这首诗是一首题壁诗,写的是诗人清晨游破山寺后禅院的观感。

Background

Chang Jian (708-765 AD), a poet in the Tang Dynasty, often visited mountains and forests after a frustrated career in politics. This poem was inscribed on a wall, describing the poet's reflections after a morning tour.

题破山寺后禅院

常 建

清晨入古寺,
初日照高林。

曲径通幽处,

禅房花木深。

山光悦鸟性,

潭影空人心。

万籁此都寂,

但余钟磬音。

A BUDDHIST RETREAT BEHIND AN OLD TEMPLE IN THE MOUNTAIN

Chang Jian

I come to the old temple at first light;

Only tree-tops are steeped in sunbeams bright.

A winding footpath leads to deep retreat;

The abbot's cell is hid 'mid flowers sweet.

In mountain's aura flying birds feel pleasure;

In shaded pool a carefree mind finds leisure.

All worldly noises are quieted here;

I only hear temple bells ringing clear.

(许渊冲译; Translated by Xu Yuanchong)

 辅助理解

tí pò shān sì hòu chán yuàn
题 破 山 寺 后 禅 院

cháng jiàn
常 建

qīng chén rù gǔ sì
清 晨 入 古 寺,

chū rì zhào gāo lín
初 日 照 高 林。

qū jìng tōng yōu chù
曲 径 通 幽 处，
chán fáng huā mù shēn
禅 房 花 木 深。
shān guāng yuè niǎo xìng
山 光 悦 鸟 性，
tán yǐng kōng rén xīn
潭 影 空 人 心。
wàn lài cǐ dōu jì
万 籁 此 都 寂，
dàn yú zhōng qìng yīn
但 余 钟 磬 音。

释义

清晨我走进这座古寺，初升的太阳照耀着森林。沿着竹林间弯弯曲曲的山道朝上走，环境越来越幽深，最后通到花丛树林深处僧人诵经的禅房。群鸟飞翔在秀美的山色之间，潭水中的倒影让人心境空灵。万物的声音都安静下来，只听得到钟磬的余音。

Paraphrase

Empty hills look pure as a recent rain refines, as dusk is falling autumn is felt in the bones. A silvery moon is shining through the pines, the limpid brooks are gurgling over the stones. Bamboos laugh out as girls from washing whirl. The lotus stirs where boats out fishing curl. The scents of spring may go; that's Nature's will. This season here attracts the noble still.

生词

1. 破山寺：指的是兴福寺，在常熟市虞山，old temple in the mountain, referring to Xingfu Temple located in Mont Yu in Changshu city。

2. 后禅院：后面的禅院。寺庙常分为前院和后院，前院供佛，后院是生活区，back hall of Buddhist temple。Temples usually have two halls. The front hall is for worshiping and the back one is for living.

3. 初日：早上的太阳，sun in the morning。

4. 悦：让……高兴，to delight。

5. 空：让……空明，to empty。

6. 钟磬：钟和磬是两种乐器，寺庙里鸣钟的意思是开始，击磬的意思是结束。Bell ringing means start while chime stone ringing means end.

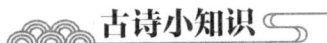 古诗小知识

题壁诗

题壁诗是一种写在墙上的诗。题壁始于两汉，盛于唐宋。题诗的墙壁一般是寺庙的墙壁，人来人往的石壁、楼壁、邮亭壁等。墙壁是诗人发表诗歌的平台，题壁诗也成为一种独特的文学和书法作品；墙壁同时也是开放的交流平台，从皇帝到百姓，不论身份的高低，人们看到墙上的诗后都可以留言和回复。

Poetry Tips

Wall Poems

Wall poems are poems inscribed on a wall. The practice began in the Han Dynasty and flourished in the Tang and Song dynasties. The walls on which poems are inscribed are generally temple walls, stone walls, building walls, courier station walls, etc. The wall poem has become a unique literary and calligraphy work. At the same time, the wall is not only a platform for poets to publish their poems, but also an open exchange platform, on which, everyone, from the Emperor to the ordinary people, regardless of their status, can leave their messages and reply after reading the poems on the wall.

 练习题

1. 填空。

《题破山寺后禅院》由（   ）句组成，每句（   ）个字，全诗一共（   ）个字。第（   ）句、第（   ）句和第（   ）句押韵。

2. 除了墙壁，酒馆也是古诗传播的平台，请找一找诗人在酒馆写的诗，看看这些诗与题壁诗各有什么特点。

3. 成语"曲径通幽"出自《题破山寺后禅院》。哪些地方可以用"曲径通幽"来形容？

拓展阅读

题 都 城 南 庄
tí dū chéng nán zhuāng

崔 护
cuī hù

去年今日此门中，
qù nián jīn rì cǐ mén zhōng

人面桃花相映红。
rén miàn táo huā xiāng yìng hóng

人面不知何处去，
rén miàn bù zhī hé chù qù

桃花依旧笑春风。
táo huā yī jiù xiào chūn fēng

题西林壁

苏轼

横看成岭侧成峰,
远近高低各不同。
不识庐山真面目,
只缘身在此山中。

黄鹤楼

崔颢

昔人已乘黄鹤去,
此地空余黄鹤楼。
黄鹤一去不复返,
白云千载空悠悠。
晴川历历汉阳树,
芳草萋萋鹦鹉洲。
日暮乡关何处是?
烟波江上使人愁。

第十五课 别

送杜少府之任蜀州

创作背景

诗人王勃（约公元650—676年）才华出众，是"初唐四杰"之一。王勃的一位朋友即将离开长安，到四川做官。王勃在长安相送，即将与朋友离别时作了这首诗。

Background

Wang Bo (c. 650-676 AD) was one of the "Four Great Poets in the Early Tang Dynasty". One of Wang Bo's friends was about to leave Chang'an for Sichuan as an official. Wang Bo wrote this poem in Chang'an when he saw his friend off.

送杜少府之任蜀州

王勃

城阙辅三秦，
风烟望五津。

与君离别意，

同是宦游人。

海内存知己，

天涯若比邻。

无为在歧路，

儿女共沾巾。

FAREWELL TO PREFECT DU

Wang Bo

You leave the town walled far and wide

For mist-veiled land by riverside.

I feel on parting sad and drear,

For both of us are strangers here.

If you have friends who know your heart,

Distance cannot keep you apart.

At crossroads where we bid adieu,

Do not shed tears as women do !

（许渊冲译；Translated by Xu Yuanchong）

sòng dù shǎo fǔ zhī rèn shǔ zhōu
送 杜 少 府 之 任 蜀 州

wáng bó
王 勃

chéng què fǔ sān qín
城 阙 辅 三 秦，

fēng yān wàng wǔ jīn
风 烟 望 五 津。

与君离别意，
同是宦游人。
海内存知己，
天涯若比邻。
无为在歧路，
儿女共沾巾。

释义

三秦大地护卫着长安城，遥望五津，一片风云烟雾。我与你离别，充满愁意，因为你我都是远离家乡外出做官的人。但是只要四海之中有了解自己的人，即使远在天涯也好像近邻。所以我们不要像男女一样泪湿手巾，在分别的岔路上悲伤。

Paraphrase

By this wall that surrounds the three Qin districts, through a mist that makes five rivers one. We bid each other a sad farewell, we two officials going opposite ways. And yet, while China holds our friendship, and heaven remains our neighborhood, why should you linger at the fork of road, wiping your eyes like a heart-broken child?

生词

1. 少府：官名，指县尉，an official just below the head of the county。
2. 之：去，to go, leave for。
3. 蜀州：也称蜀川，今四川崇州，also known as Shuchuan, the present-day Chongzhou in Sichuan Province。
4. 城阙：长安的城楼，the gate and tower of Chang'an。
5. 辅：护卫，to protect。

6. 三秦：长安附近的关中地区。秦朝（公元前 221—前 206 年）灭亡后，项羽把关中分为三个部分，分给秦朝的三个投降的将军，所以关中也被称为三秦。Guanzhong, the neighborhood of Chang'an. After the fall of the Qin Dynasty in 206 BC, Xiang Yu divided it into three parts and awarded them to three generals who surrendered.

7. 五津：岷江的五个渡口，这里泛指蜀川，five ferries on the Min River. Here it refers to Shuchuan.

8. 宦游：离开家乡，到外地做官，to leave home and take up government employments。

9. 海内：四海之内，指全国各地，throughout the country。

10. 天涯：天边，非常远的地方，skyline, a faraway place。

11. 比邻：近邻，next-door neighbor。

12. 无为：不必，do not have to。

13. 歧路：分岔的路，古代人常在大路的分岔处告别，branch road where ancient people usually say goodbye。

14. 沾巾：弄湿手巾，指流泪，to get the handkerchief wet。Here it refers to shedding tears.

古诗小知识

海 内

《送少府之任蜀州》中"海内存知己"的"海内"指的是中国。这里的"海"是"四海"，源于"文命，敷于四海"（《尚书·大禹谟》）。古代人认为中国四周都是海，因此称"中国"为"海内"。

Poetry Tips

Hainei (Within the Seas)

"海内" (within the seas) in *Farewell to Prefect Du* refers to the whole China. "海" means "sea" in Chinese and here it refers to the "four seas", a term derived from "文命，敷于四海" ("Only a moderate decree can be widely applied everywhere")

(*The Book of History: Da Yu*). The ancient people thought that China was surrounded by four seas, so they called "China" within the seas.

练习题

1. 填空。

《送杜少府之任蜀州》由（　　）句组成，每句（　　）个字，全诗一共（　　）个字。第（　　）句、第（　　）句和第（　　）句押韵。

2.《送少府之任蜀州》是一首送别诗，人们送别的时候一般有什么样的感受？"海内存知己啊，天涯若比邻"表达的是什么样的感受？

3. 假如你要做一个毕业离别发言，跟你的中文老师、中国同学告别，请写一个简短的发言稿。发言稿中要用学过的一句诗来表达你的感受。

 拓展阅读

送柴侍御
王昌龄

流水通波接武冈,
送君不觉有离伤。
青山一道同云雨,
明月何曾是两乡。

别董大(其一)
高适

千里黄云白日曛,
北风吹雁雪纷纷。
莫愁前路无知己,
天下谁人不识君?

宣州谢朓楼饯别校书叔云
李白

弃我去者,昨日之日不可留;
乱我心者,今日之日多烦忧。

长风万里送秋雁,对此可以酣高楼。
蓬莱文章建安骨,中间小谢又清发。
俱怀逸兴壮思飞,欲上青天览明月。
抽刀断水水更流,举杯消愁愁更愁。
人生在世不称意,明朝散发弄扁舟。

汉英对照词汇表

A
暗香　a delicate fragrance

B
报　to repay
比邻　next-door neighbor
泊　to moor
不平　unfair; unjust

C
苍苍　lush and green
曾　to emerge in an endless stream
慈母　loving, caring mother
城阙　the gate and tower of Chang'an
愁　worry; sadness
初日　sun in the morning
处处　everywhere
春芳　spring flowers
寸草　young grass

D
岱宗　another name for Mount Tai as principal of the Five Great Mountains

荡胸　to broad the mind
得　to get

F
发生　to rain
缝　to stitch, to sew
夫如何　how about
辅　to protect

G
割昏晓　to divide north from south, dusk from dawn
个　this
故乡　hometown, native place, birthplace
归　to go back to
桂花　osmanthus flowers

H
海内　throughout the country
寒梅　plum blossoms
荷　to carry on one's shoulder or back
后禅院　back hall of Buddhist temple
浣　to wash clothes
宦游　to leave home and take up government employments
晖　sunshine
会当　must
火炉　heating stove

J
涧　creek, ravine
剑　long sword with double-edged blade
锦官城　another name for Chengdu

惊　to startle

俱　all

决眦　to keep eyes open

君　you

K

客　person engaged in some particular pursuit

空　to empty

旷　vast, spacious

L

来日　past days

笠　bamboo or straw hat with a conical crown and broad brim, to shelter one from the sun and rain

临行　before leaving

凌　to face defiantly

绿蚁　green ants

M

梅花　mume blossoms

密密　tight, close

眠　to sleep

暝　dusk

明镜　bright mirror. It also indicates that the river is like a bright mirror.

磨　to polish, to grind

N

乃　so

泥　mud, clay

P
醅　unfiltered wine

Q
绮窗　beautifully decorated window
齐鲁　two states during Spring and Autumn Period (770–476 BC)
歧路　branch road where ancient people usually say goodbye
潜　secretly, quietly, silently
墙角　corner formed by two walls
青山　green mountain
青未了　endless mountains
秋霜　autumn frost, white hair

R
刃　edges (of a knife, sword, etc.); blades
日暮　nightfall, dusk
入归鸟　saw homing birds
润　to moisten

S
三春　sān chūn
三千丈　extremely long
三秦　Guanzhong, the neighborhood of Chang'an
上人　an honorific form for Buddhist monk
少府　an official just below the head of the county
神秀　magical and beautiful view
时　every now and then, at times
示　to show
蜀州　also known as Shuchuan, the present-day Chongzhou in Sichuan Province
数　several, a few

霜　white hoar

似　to be similar

宿　to stay overnight

T

啼　(of certain birds and animals) to sing, to twitter

天涯　skyline, a faraway place

W

晚来　night fall

王孙　offspring of the nobility, here referring to hermit

望岳　to look up at Mount Tai

为　because

未　(used at the end of questions, indicating doubt) or not

未曾　never before, haven't

闻　to hear

无　question word for yes-no questions

无为　do not have to

五津　five ferries on the Min River

X

晓　dawn, daybreak

斜阳　setting sun

喧　clamor

Y

烟　mist

阳　*Yang* refers to the south of the mountain.

杳杳　deep and somber

遥　distant, far away

野　wilderness, open country, field

野径　track in the wilderness

夜来　last night

移　to move, to paddle

意恐　to worry

阴　*Yin* refers to the north of the mountain.

吟　song, a type of classical poetry

游子　person traveling or living far from home

欲　about to, going to

缘　because, for (reason)

悦　to delight

Z

杂诗　similar to the poems without titles but with a wide range of subjects

造化　nature

沾巾　to get the handkerchief wet

枝　measure word for flowers with stems intact

之　to go, to leave for

钟　bell

钟　to concentrate

钟磬　bell ringing means start while chime stone ringing means end

舟　boat

渚　islet

著花　to blossom

诗人索引

第一课

王安石(公元 1021—1086 年),字介甫,北宋(公元 960—1127 年)诗人,北宋宋神宗年间(公元 1067—1085 年)曾任宰相。

Wang Anshi (1021-1086 AD), courtesy name Jiefu, was a poet of the Northern Song Dynasty (960-1127 AD). He served as the prime minister during Emperor Shenzong of Song period (1067-1085 AD).

王冕(公元 1310—1359 年),字元章,元代(1271—1368 年)画家和诗人,擅长画梅花。

Wang Mian (1310-1359 AD), courtesy name Yuanzhang, was a poet and a painter who specialised in mume blossom paintings during the Yuan Dynasty (1271-1368 AD).

第二课

孟浩然(公元 689—740 年),唐代(公元 618—907 年)山水田园派诗人。

Meng Haoran (689-740 AD), was a Tang Dynasty (618-907 AD) poet who gained prominence for landscape poetry.

杜甫(公元 712—770 年),字子美,唐代(公元 618—907 年)现实主义诗人,被称为"诗圣",他的诗被称为"诗史"。

Du Fu (712-770 AD), courtesy name Zimei, was a poet of the Tang Dynasty (618-907 AD). His poetry shows a concern for the society and the underprivileged. The Chinese often refer to him as the *Poet Sage* and the *Poet Historian*.

朱熹（公元 1130—1200 年），字元晦，南宋（公元 1127—1279 年）诗人。

Zhu Xi (1130-1200 AD), also known by his courtesy name Yuanhui, was a poet of the Southern Song Dynasty (1127-1279 AD).

李白（公元 701—762 年），字太白，唐代（公元 618—907 年）浪漫主义诗人，被称为"诗仙"。

Li Bai (701-762 AD), courtesy name Taibai, was a poet who lived during the Tang Dynasty (618-907 AD). Being called the *Poet Immortal*, Li Bai was a romantic in his verse.

第三课

孟浩然（见第二课）。

苏轼（公元 1037—1101 年），字子瞻，也被称为苏东坡，北宋（公元 960—1127 年）诗人。

Su Shi (1037-1101 AD), courtesy name Zizhan, also being called Su Dongpo, was a poet of the Northern Song Dynasty (960-1127 AD).

李白（见第二课）。

白居易（公元 772—846 年），字乐天，唐代（公元 618—907 年）现实主义诗人。

Bai Juyi (772-846 AD), courtesy name Letian, was a realistic poet of the Tang Dynasty (618-907 AD).

第四课

王维（公元 701—761 年），字摩诘，唐代（公元 618—907 年）山水田园诗人，被称为"诗佛"。

Wang Wei (701-761 AD), courtesy name Mojie, was a landscape poet during the Tang Dynasty (618-907 AD). He was referred to as the *Poet Buddha*.

韦应物（公元 737—792 年），字义博，唐代（公元 618—907 年）山水田园诗人。

Wei Yingwu (737-792 AD), courtesy name Yibo, was a landscape poet of the Tang Dynasty (618-907 AD).

杜甫（见第二课）。

欧阳修(公元1007—1072年),字永叔,北宋(公元960—1127年)诗人。

Ouyang Xiu (1007-1072 AD), courtesy name Yongshu, was a poet of the Northern Song Dynasty (960-1127 AD).

第五课

刘长卿(公元718—790年),字文房,唐代(公元618—907年)诗人。

Liu Zhangqing (718-790 AD), courtesy name Wenfang, was a poet during the Tang Dynasty (618-907 AD).

王维(见第四课)。

李白(见第二课)。

第六课

贾岛(公元779—843年),字阆仙,唐代(公元618—907年)诗人。

Jia Dao (779-843 AD), courtesy name Langxian, was a poet active during the Tang Dynasty (618-907 AD).

白居易(见第三课)。

崔融(公元653—706年),字安成,唐代(公元618—907年)诗人。

Cui Rong (653-706 AD), courtesy name Ancheng, was a poet of the Tang Dynasty (618-907 AD).

骆宾王(约公元626—687年),字观光,唐代(公元618—907年)诗人。

Luo Binwang (c. 626-687 AD), courtesy name Guanguang, was a poet of the Tang Dynasty (618-907 AD).

第七课

王维(见第四课)。

贺知章(公元659—744年),字季真,唐代(公元618—907年)诗人。

He Zhizhang (659-744 AD), courtesy name Jizhen, was a poet of the Tang Dynasty (618-907 AD).

第八课

李白(见第二课)。

陈子昂（约公元659—700年），字伯玉，唐代（公元618—907年）诗人。

Chen Ziang (c. 659-700 AD), courtesy name Boyu, was a Chinese poet of the Tang Dynasty (618-907 AD).

李煜（公元937—978年），字重光，南唐（公元937—975年）末代君主，也被称为"南唐后主"。

Li Yu (937-978 AD), courtesy name Chongguang, was the last ruler of the Southern Tang Kingdom (937-975 AD), also known as *the Latter Lord of Southern Tang*.

第九课

白居易（见第三课）。

赵师秀（公元1170—1219年），字紫芝，南宋（公元1127—1279年）诗人。

Zhao Shixiu (1170-1219 AD), courtesy name Zizhi, was a poet of the Southern Song Dynasty (1127-1279 AD).

杜甫（见第二课）。

孟浩然（见第二课）。

第十课

孟郊（公元751—814年），字东野，唐代（公元618—907年）诗人。

Meng Jiao (751-814 AD) , courtesy name Dongye, was a poet of the Tang Dynasty (618-907 AD).

蒋士铨（公元1725—1785年），字心馀，清代（公元1616—1911年）诗人。

Jiang Shiquan (1725-1785 AD), courtesy name Xinyu, was a Qing Dynasty (1616-1911 AD) poet.

李商隐（公元约813—858年），字义山，唐代（公元618—907年）诗人。

Li Shangyin (813-858 AD), courtesy name Yishan, was a poet of the Tang Dynasty (618-907 AD).

王冕（见第一课）。

第十一课

杜甫（见第二课）。

李白(见第二课)。

第十二课

杜甫(见第二课)。

李商隐(见第十课)。

韩愈(公元 768—824 年),字退之,唐代(公元 618—907 年)诗人。

Han Yu (768-824 AD), courtesy name Tuizhi, was a poet of the Tang Dynasty (618-907 AD).

许浑(公元约 791—约 858 年),字用晦,唐代(公元 618—907 年)诗人。

Xu Hun (c. 791-858 AD), courtesy name Yonghui, was a poet of the Tang Dynasty (618-907 AD).

第十三课

王维(见第四课)。

温庭筠(约公元约 812—866 年),字飞卿,唐代(公元 618—907 年)诗人。

Wen Tingyun (c. 812-866 AD), courtesy name Feiqing, was a poet during the Tang Dynasty (618-907 AD).

第十四课

常建(公元 708—765 年),字少府,唐代(公元 618—907 年)诗人。

Chang Jian (708-765 AD), courtesy name Shaofu, was a poet during the Tang Dynasty (618-907 AD).

崔护(公元 772—846 年),字殷功,唐代(公元 618—907 年)诗人。

Cui Hu (772-846 AD), courtesy name Yingong, was a poet of the Tang Dynasty (618-907 AD).

苏轼(见第三课)。

崔颢(704—754 年),唐代(公元 618—907 年)诗人。

Cui Hao (704-754 AD) was a poet of the Tang Dynasty (618-907 AD).

第十五课

王勃(约公元 650—676 年),字子安,唐代(公元 618—907 年)诗人。

Wang Bo (c. 650-676 AD), courtesy name Zian, was a poet of the Tang Dynasty (618-907 AD).

王昌龄(公元698—757年),字少伯,唐代(公元618—907年)边塞诗人。

Wang Changling (698-757 AD), courtesy name Shaobo, was a Frontier poet of the Tang Dynasty (618-907 AD).

高适(公元704—765年),字达夫,唐代(公元618—907年)边塞诗人。

Gao Shi (704-765 AD), courtesy name Dafu, was a Frontier poet of the Tang Dynasty (618-907 AD).

李白(见第二课)。